# Santa Daddy

## LIBBY SCORES

Santa Daddy

Copyright © 2024

All rights reserved.

Book Cover by Elizabeth Scozzari

Fifth edition 2025

ISBN: 979-8-9987816-3-6

❀ Formatted with Vellum

# Content Warning

*To everyone who has ever wanted to be on Santa's naughty list*

*—*

*ho, ho, ho!*

# One

I suppress a groan as the oversized elf yells, "NEXT."

Before I can even make my way forward, my little brother shoulder checks me on his way toward the exit.

"Oh no you don't," I say.

His windbreaker shushes under my grip. Apparently he's officially reached the age where it's uncool to believe and even less cool to hang out with your sister at the mall. Not that my plans include on sitting on the old man's lap cooing like I'm still in middle school, but when I follow Sebastian's eyes I understand why his cheeks are redder than Santa's hat. A few of the friends he's meeting after this are walking toward the spectacle.

I tug on his sleeve pulling him closer to the big man. Sebastian groans.

"Sabby," his voice low and strained. "Do I *have to*?"

I shift my focus back to my brother.

"Yes," I say.

Probably louder than necessary, but I want to make sure that his dorky friend heard loud and clear.

"I promised Susan. Plus Dad said there'd be a new game thing in it for you."

I turn my head back toward Santa with both Sebastian and

my pride in tow before sitting down. His eyes bore into mine, bringing the smell of pine cones to my nose.

"Sorry Santa," I said, "you'll just have to get him something else."

His knee's surprisingly boney for a large man. Then I remember the stuffing probably comes with the suit. The effortless way he bounces me suggests he's definitely still spry. Then he whispers in my ear.

"Ho, ho ho." His gruff voice scratched against my skin.

It isn't until then that I look beyond the costume and to his actual face. His eyes are a deep hazel green like a forest of pine trees. His skin, whatever is visible behind the well groomed, oversized Santa beard is a little creased around the eyes, but smooth and clear. I think about how it will feel beneath my hand.

Heat presses against my back awakening a slew of tingles down my spine. It's his, *Santa's*, hand. His fingers touch my side; easily covering the small of my back. I shift. His thigh hardens underneath my ass. He has to be made of muscles.

"Come on Sebastian, other kids are waiting. Let's go," I say. "Santa is a very busy man, lots of joy to spread."

His grip tightens around me. It's only there for a moment along with a naughty twinkle in his eyes. I think about what I just said. My cheeks redden. *Lots of joy to spread.* I shift my gaze over to my brother, who finally resigns onto the big man's other knee with a dramatic sigh.

"So Bastian," Santa's voice booms, "your sister tells me you've been a good boy this year. Has she been a good girl?"

More shivers run down my back. Am I really getting turned on by this old man? A ripped old man with clear skin and magical eyes.

"No," Sebastian said. "She hasn't. Our parents were happy she turned 21 because they figured it was one less thing they had to worry about her getting busted for."

"SEBASTIAN," I whisper, an edge creeping to my voice. "It

was a joke, clearly one not meant for eleven year olds," I say, turning to Santa.

Santa laughs, shaking both of us on his knee.

"Over here," the photographer calls out. "Say SLEIGH RIDE!"

Both Sebastian and I look over. My skin feels tight across my face. I'm sure if I'm grimacing or smiling. The laughter from my brother and Santa is rubbing off on me, and I feel my features relax. I'm smiling now, though I'm not sure if it's from happiness or from thinking of a different kind of ride I'd like to take with Santa.

The pictures will make both our parents happy. It's the kind of picture, Susan, Sebastian's mom and my stepmom, will print out in a hundred different formats over the years, the kind that will be included in both of our graduation ceremonies—mine next year, Sebastian's middle school one in the not too far off future.

"Now, what do want for Christmas?" Santa repeats to Sebastian.

"Other than the new—" he starts.

"Yes," Santa nods.

Sebastian lifts his hand and waves his fingers drawing Santa in like he has some big secret. Santa leans forward and tilts his head. Regardless of where his face is, those damn eyes are angled up at me. My body tightens and heats at my core. In the middle of the mall, I can see that beard splayed out over my thighs.

"That's a lovely Christmas wish," Santa says.

His full, pink lips push through his beard into a smile. Can he feel me, hot and wet on top of his lap? *This will be the last time I ever sit on a mall Santa's lap*, I scold myself internally.

"And for you, Sabby?"

My name sounds like heaven coming from those beautiful lips. There are a lot of things I want in this moment, namely him. I swallow, nearly choking on my own spit.

"Whatever you give me is more than enough."

I'm trying to keep my face in some sort of smile. *Lame, so lame.*

"Come on, Sebastian," I say. "We have to get going now."

"Bye Santa," he whispers

"Merry Christmas," Santa bellows.

The dash to the exit is short. Sebastian's able to avoid his friends and I managed to not say anything desperately stupid to the mall Santa, who is about the same age as my dad, if I have to guess. Not that I care about age gaps. My dad was already widowed and in his 40s when he met Susan, unwed and in her 30s. When they had my brother I was already 10. None of it changes how I feel about the little guy or Susan. They're my family.

And Susan is going to be jazzed about the picture. I show it to Sebastian, who agrees. We all look great: my brother, me, and that red-suited devil.

"Must have been a Christmas miracle. You're headed to Game Stop to meet your friends?"

"No, Sabby! We're meeting at BK in the food court *then* we're going to Game Stop."

I can hear the eye roll, even though I can't see it. The proof that the kid is my brother through and through.

"Well, get going before they give away all of the crowns to the other little kids," I tease.

"You're so lame," he says.

I watch him as he turns in the direction of the escalator.

"All part of being an older sister. Seriously Bastian, be careful and I'll meet you at the Starbucks in four hours. Got it?"

"Yes *mom!*"

His sticks his tongue out before running off. The kid's a goober sometimes, but he's my goober.

"Now to get to Game Stop before they sell out of those consoles," I say to myself.

*Two*

Thankfully I had gotten there just in time. They had three left and only two after I checked out. Christmas miracles indeed. I just relax into my seat at the high tops near the bar when Emma jumps out from no where.

"Gahhh," I say, catching the menu as it slips from my hands. "Are you still going to be doing that when we're in our 80s?"

"Absolutely," my best friend from high school says.

We had made plans to grab a drink or two while my brother was off galavanting the mall with his friends. Four hours was enough time to teeter on the edge of buzzed before being sober enough to responsibly drive home.

We decide on a charcuterie board and two glasses of a buttery Chardonnay. The saltiness of the cured meats tickles my tongue. For a moment I wonder if Santa's sack would have a similar taste.

"SABBY?!"

Emma's snapping fingers jolt me back to reality.

"What?"

"What are you thinking about?" She asks.

"Nothing. . ."

I let my voice trail off. There really isn't anything.

"Nothing my ass," she says before polishing off her glass of Chardonnay. "That's the look you get when you're thinking about a guy."

My eyes roll at her cooing.

"Seriously Emma, it's nothing. There's no one."

The waiter comes over. I breathe a small sigh of relief. I'm not good at hiding things, part of the reason Sebastian's comment to Santa is only partly a joke. I can get things by our parents better, but I'm especially shit at hiding anything from Emma. While there's nothing to tell, I'm still having mixed feelings about my earlier encounter with Santa.

Who got their jollies off to Old Saint Nick? Especially in the form of mall Santas. Not that I've gotten off. Maybe later those hazel eyes would be reflected back at me when I—

"Sabby? You in?"

"Of course!"

*Shit*, I have no idea what I just agreed to. I flash my brightest smile topped with wink at Emma and the waiter. It's all in the sell, sometimes, if I can sell it.

"Yay!" Emma claps.

The waiter smiles and walks away.

"So, while you were totally daydreaming about No One," Emma presses, "our waiter closed our check since he's off shift."

I knock back the rest of my wine, and smirk. Knowing Emma there's more to the story.

"And he'll come back to join us momentarily," she laughs. "Fair game?"

I nod.

"Standard rules?"

"Five minutes, open flirting. Whoever he shows more interest in after that has first dibs."

Emma winks and breaks into an evil laugh at something behind me. Before I turn around a small tray with five shots is hovering near my face being placed down on the table.

"Emma," I groan. "I have to drive."

"Not for another three hours. Besides, you've had one glass of wine. Here," she says, handing me a piece of bread. "Shoot your shot and carb load."

I take the bread and pluck one of the shots from the tray.

"Tequila?"

"The things I do for you," Emma says. Her voice is extra breathy.

Her gaze wanders up the body of the waiter.

"Well," she leans further across the table, her face tilting up as her mouth hovers at the level of his belt buckle, "Dylan. Are you going to make yourself comfortable?"

The way she asks would have been better suited if we were at her off campus apartment instead of a bar. Dylan pulls out a chair to join us.

"To jingle bells and ho, ho, hos," Emma says, lifting a shot glass.

"To new friends," I add, reaching my hand out toward Dylan.

"The more the merrier," he chimes in.

The kid was certainly ballsy, he's aware of the innuendo. It wouldn't be the first time Emma and I play in each other's sandbox, there are ways this game can end in a tie, but only if player three is exceptional. Dylan is just another guy.

I keep playing along, letting Emma and Dylan take the second shots. It's clear he is way more into Emma than me. Besides, I'm not into it. Every time I thought of something over the top flirty, that gruff voice fills my head: *has she been a good girl?*

Dylan excuses himself to go to the bathroom, clearly excited at the prospect of heading out with Emma. I watch as he turns the corner, before he's disappeared from sight Emma is leaning forward eyeing me like a cat near a fish bowl.

"Congrats on the win," I say, nodding. "We'll grab the check and then I'll say my goodbyes?"

"Later tonight I'll call you for more information on No One.

I've never seen you throw a challenge outside of high school gym, and certainly never a round of Fair Game."

Before I can protest, or even remember that ladies with nothing to hide don't protest *too* much, Emma fills her glass and pours the last of the wine in mine.

"Already paid the check." She waves her hand, adding, "and the tip. You get breakfast this Sunday. We'll swap stories?"

Dylan reappears around the bend a few tables away.

"Fine. Quick over or under."

"What's your guess?"

I sigh rolling my eyes trying to remember anything Dylan had said.

"A strong five."

"I'm going over," Emma whispers.

"Wishful thinking or do you know something I don't?"

We're both on the brink of tears as Dylan stops next to the hightop.

"Seems like I missed something good," he say, still standing.

"Depends on who you ask," I say. "It was lovely to meet you Dylan."

I pick up my wine glass and in two swallows it's gone. Emma stands up at the same time and we exchange a round of hugs and pleasantries.

"Em, your wine!"

My finger pointing accusingly at the near full glass. Our tit-for-tat drinking has gotten both of us in a lot of trouble and I'm not letting her start making better decisions now.

"Oh, it's okay."

Her voice comes out sounding the most like a fairytale princess I've ever heard.

"I'll sit with you, if you wanted to finish it?"

"That would be great, Dylan. If you don't mind?"

He shakes his head. His dirty blonde shag swaying with the motion.

"You guys have fun! Bye!"

I push my chair in, making sure I take the gaming console and my purse, then walk away. I'm not a few feet away when I hear Emma's familiar giggle.

*At least one of us will be getting laid.* I'm pretty sure all of my things are still at school. Who comes home for the holidays and packs their sex toys? I glance down at my hands, my fingers wrapped around the bag holding a present for my brother. God blessed me with ten fingers and I plan to use at least four of them later.

Unfortunately, in addition to sex, I'm now craving a cigarette. *Damn wine.* The cold is bracing, but I turn and go back into the mall entrance. There's a no smoking policy in Dad and Susan's house. It's one of the few rules I don't break since my mom died of lung cancer. She had never smoked a single cigarette a day in her life. I didn't plan on being a smoker forever, but social smoking in college has been fun. After sex it is never a let down either.

I still have two hours before I meet up with Bastian. We're supposed to grab hot chocolate and then have an impromptu drive around town to look at the Christmas lights. I've been around the block long enough to know our parents are planning some crazy Christmas surprise, but I don't think Bastian knows. I smile to myself. Thankfully everyone is so absorbed in their own holiday hecticity I'm sure no one notices.

I stop and buy cigarettes from the convenience store on the second floor. As I tuck the pack into my purse I realize I could have swung by my car to see if there were any stashed in the glove compartment. The few slices of prosciutto and cubes of cheddar along with the one piece of bread I had weren't holding up to the two glasses of wine and a shot of tequila.

If Emma was here we would be walking and laughing, window shopping and picking up for last minute gifts—which is how I do most of my Christmas shopping—I'd be too distracted to realize how horny I was. Or she would tease me relentlessly until we ended up in Spencer's picking through the various toy options.

The cigarettes in my hand are calling to me. I look up and see that the entrance where we came in is close. I'll sneak out, have a quick smoke, then do a wash up outside of my car. My essential oils body spray lives in my center console. I start walking over. The line for pictures is still wrapped around the corner. Just what I need, another glance at Mall Santa. It has definitely been too long since I last had sex. What other explanation was there for the wetness between my legs?

I exhaled a breath I wasn't aware I was holding as I walk by and see Santa's on his break. His chair is empty and there's a North Pole looking sign that says he'll be back in a bit. My shoulders and my abs relax. Not that I feel like I have to suck my stomach, nor would I even if I did, but since I can't lay down in the middle of the mall and arch my back just enough to give the illusion that my barely B cups are really C cups — my hand slaps against my forehead like I forgot something. Must have been my brain. I'm not even home yet and I'm starting a fantasy. *Tequila.*

It's not like Emma knew it had been a minute, but that's not stopping me from ordering the fluffiest, butteriest, most glorious pancakes she can't have when we go out to breakfast. Evil is as evil does.

I make my way out of the door. It's one of those weird entrances and exits that former mall employees and people who are only stopping in for the restrooms seem to know about or use. Those days at the candle store still haunt my olfactory senses.

There's no one around, which is both good and bad. It's still early enough that streaks of sunlight are holding back the dusk. I check my key ring—my pepper spray is nowhere to be seen. Probably in my nightstand drawer next to my cigarettes and Willie Nelson, my half glass, half silicone s-shaped vibrator. Everyone has favorites.

I open the trunk, popping the game console in underneath a

blanket that's been back here from at least two boyfriends ago. Hopefully the flaky white stain I left facing outward would deter any thieves. They don't need to know it's actually from a glazed donut.

The wind feels cold against my teeth. I stop smiling and unlock the passenger's side door. Unlike the big candy apple red truck next to the driver's side, there's no one parked on this side of my car and it's easier to dig through the junk that's accumulated in the glove box and center console.

Underneath a bundle of napkins I see my spray and one white and gold box. There are three cigarettes in the pack.

"Double score," I say under my breath.

I go to put the napkins back in the glove compartment but they're hard. Like something stuffed inside them hard.

It would probably be smart to throw it out, whatever *it* is, but my curiosity has already gotten the better of me. Each layer crinkles a little as I peel it back. It's like whatever was put inside had been wet or maybe dried off with the napkins and then shoved in the box. I take a stilted breath and cross my toes.

It could be—it is. Masturbating might not be hockey, but this is the hat trick of Christmas miracles. There in the middle of the napkins is the small teardrop shaped vibrator this girl got me. We were going on a first date to some action-adventure-superhero movie that Bastian probably would have enjoyed more, and she handed me a small wrapped box. I rocked the device, she manned the remote, and it was probably the most fun I've ever had on a first date at the movies. We lasted about as long as the movie. Maybe when I get back to school I'll give her a call. See if she's seeing anyone; if she is, I can ask if they want a third for the night?

My eyes roll. I'm ridiculous. My purse and the pack of cigarettes are sitting on the seat, and I'm wiping the vibrator down with new napkins and the water bottle I swore I would actually drink.

I slide into the passenger seat, moving my stuff to the floor, and close the door behind me. I didn't even check to see if the damn thing was charged before unbuttoning my jeans. I'm not sure where the remote is, but I can find it later. If I remember correctly there's a button that powers the device on if you double tap it.

Oh god, it still works. It takes a few minutes to position it exactly where I want it. It's not life changing, but it will definitely help push me over the edge I seem to be hanging out on today. A car door closes nearby.

The device is made to be remote, I laugh to myself. The buzzing muffles as I zip and button my jeans. I'll walk over to the smoking section, have a quick cigarette, and then hit the bathrooms to clean up. If I haven't gotten off by then, I'll take this baby for a walk around the mall. Santa flashes in my mind, sitting in his oversized chair, bouncing his knee as if he's waiting for me.

I go to open the door and the pattern of the vibrations changes. My breath catches. It's still a setting or two away from the one I like best if I remember correctly. But I thought I needed the—

Outside of my door there is a person in a black and red coat pressing the button on a bright pink remote. With every movement of his finger the pattern in my panties changes. I stifle a moan as the device shakes against me, caressing my clit at just the right angle. I don't want to move, but I am not having my orgasm manipulated by a stranger.

I open the car door and slide out. The stranger is now aware of the movement and turns.

On second thought, if a stranger was going to ring my bell, it would have to be this one. Tall, jacked, with a bone structure Greek gods would kill for. His lips are full and his eyes are dark swirls, mostly his pupil has pushed the color right from them.

"Um, hi," I say, caught off guard. "That's my remote. That you're holding."

He looks between me and the remote. He presses the button

again and the vibrating intensifies. The only sounds I hear are my breathing, straining to not be completely erratic, and the hum of delight.

"Oh," his voice is gravelly.

Not like a smoker's, but like someone who has been presenting all day. The way my old lit professor used to sound when he would teach five classes in a row and then have our advisor meeting, which he always pushed back to Friday's at 4:30 pm. Happy hour indeed.

I'm trying to keep it together, but it feels so good. I watch as his eyes travel down from my face to my pussy and back up. I feel the color rising to my face with his gaze. The pressure is building. It's really been a minute and there's something about this man, watching, knowing.

"You probably want it back then," his voice lingers.

He goes to hand it to me, the plastic is hard but smooth compared to his rough, tattooed fingers. The button clicks and I accidentally grab his hand instead of taking the remote from him.

A small moan catches in my throat. I try to speak but I don't trust myself in this moment. I look up at him, into his eyes. They are gorgeous, and so familiar. Before I can recall where I know this man from the soft/hard, slow/fast/pause vibrations start taking over.

"I could give you an orgasm for Christmas, Sabby, but if I'm going to do that there are other ways I'd like to."

Recognition seeps in between the small waves of pleasure cresting.

"Santa?"

He nods. His 5 o'clock shadow glistens in the dying sunlight and the dark ruffles of his hair move softly.

"Would you like me to give you your Christmas jollies, Sabby?"

I remember how his hand felt on my back, the strength of his leg as he bounced me. He was sexy as Santa and is hot as fuck out of costume.

"Yes, please."

My voice is barely audible.

He clicks the button. Whether it was the timing or the setting I like, I feel like I'm going to — it stops. I pull my eyes away from his and down to his hand. His finger is still holding the button.

"It's too bad you're on the naughty list, Sabby. Would you like to try to be a good girl instead?"

I feel myself dripping.

"Yes," I whisper.

"Yes, Santa," he corrects.

He takes my hand and guides me flush against the door of my car. With his fingers still laced through mine, he uses his other hand to pop the button and free the zipper on my jeans. His fingers tease me as they skate right above my flesh, between the damp cotton of my thong and my slit, without touching me he removes the device.

"We won't be needing this. Only good girls get toys and you're not a good girl are you?"

I shake my head, breathing slowly and deeply through my mouth.

"No, Santa."

"Maybe we can change that," he winks and lets go of my hand.

My pants are fastened and he's standing before me. From the glaring bulge in front of me, I would say Santa is going to utterly destroy my stocking when he goes to stuff it.

We close up my car, I remember to lock the trunk, at least I think I do, and we walk back into the mall. Instead of heading straight into the chaos of shoppers, he takes my hand and we walk through the employee only door and into the secret hallways of the building.

I'm in trouble. I would follow this man just about anywhere. I take a breath and realize that I am, but it's hard not to. From the moment by butt planted itself onto his knee there's been a pull. Maybe it's the magic of Christmas or I really do have a thing for authority figures, I'm not sure.

Trailing behind him has given me time to really take in what I'm seeing. Underneath that red and black coat are dark blue bootcut jeans that his ass and toned thighs are trying to break free of and a waffled long sleeved shirt. He looked more like a construction worker in a porno than a mall Santa.

We get to small closet, the chatter from a crowd of people outside echoes in the hidden hallway. I wondered if we're close to Santa's workshop.

He slides a key from his pocket and unlocks the door. It's a small dressing area with an even smaller bathroom. Hanging from the door is a large, beefy black bag.

"Sabby," his voice somehow lower than before. "Do you know how girls like you end up on the naughty list?"

I watch him as he moves around the room. He hangs his coat on a nearby hook. His leather work boots, probably steel toed, are off and tucked neatly under the rack. His fingers work his belt buckle.

"No," I say mesmerized.

"To start it's the brash sense of independence. You sat on my lap, told me what you wanted for Christmas, and before I could give it to you, you tried to take it for yourself."

His breath washes over the back of my neck sending chills down my spine. I hear the soft crumple of jeans behind me, the clanking of his belt hitting the floor.

Something velvety brushes against the back of my hand. It's hard and warm. It pulses against me. As I turned my head to look, something soft touches the side of my face directing it to look the other way.

The side of his fingers drag across my bottom lip. I want to turn my hand, to feel his cock throb in my grip. Somehow I

know better. He'll tell me when I can. The ache of delayed grati-
fication pounds in my chest, in my panties.

I exhale as softly as I can, shuddering as his hand moves
down my arm.

"I *was* going to give it to you."

His fingernails push into my clavicle. My breath comes in
sharp. I push my body against his, feeling him hard, digging
into my back. I try to stand on my tiptoes, but he keeps me
steady.

"I want to give it to you, Sabby. I want to reward you for
being a good girl, but first you have to prove to me you are."

I nod. His nose presses through my hair into my scalp. His
lips touch the skin of my neck like a whisper.

He leans in further, the full size of his body pressing against
mine, wrapping around me like a cloak. His voice is still deep
but without the steel and growl of before.

"If it—if I—get to be too much, just say 'red.' Okay?"

I nod again. This time my shoulders dance as I shiver. This
man is like a searing hot flame and a heating pad at the same
time.

"Close your eyes and tell me what you were thinking about
earlier when you popped that cheap piece of plastic inside that
wet pussy."

My voice wavers for a second as I feel the space between the
two of us growing cold.

"I was thinking about the girl who gave it to me."

I feel him closer again now. His fingers brush my hair over
my shoulder and down the front of my chest. He is unbuttoning
my shirt.

"If you stop talking, I stop."

That's the last thing in the world I want.

"I was thinking about calling her to see if she wanted to hang
out."

The buttons are open on my shirt, there are only three and
they're a bitch to close, but it's one of my favorite shirts. Perfect

for pictures with Santa. His fingers are gently tugging the material up out of the band of my high waisted jeans.

"And before that?"

His voice drips into my ear and I can feel every unspoken word between us. Somehow he knew. He stops, holding my shirt under my breasts. The chilled air from the room making my nipples perk up.

I can't quite remember what exactly I was thinking before.

"Nothing really—"

A sharp stinging crosses the side of my ass cheek and I can feel it jiggle back into place. The stinging settling in.

"I saw you," his voice rumbles against my ear. "In the parking lot, searching for something. What had you so turned on, so dripping that you needed release in that instance?"

Slickness builds between my legs. Knowing he was watching makes me want him even more. My back is still arched from the smack across my ass. I've never begged before and if he doesn't touch me soon. I might start.

"I wasn't searching for the vibrator until I thought I had found it."

His hand envelops the side of my ass he spanked and he begins to rub it. Chills break out across my body. Every part of me is tingling for him. Not wanting it to stop, I continue.

"I had a few glasses of wine and a shot of tequila. I kept seeing these stunning green eyes and feeling strong hands across my back."

My voice feels as breathy as it sounds, filled with an almost painful desire. His hand keeps caressing my ass sliding up and over the ridge of my jeans, dipping his fingers under the waistband, teasing me. With his other hand he pulls my shirt over my head and drops it on the floor. I tilt my head back and rest it on his muscular chest.

The textured flesh of his calloused hands tease the sensitive part of my nipples and tickle the skin around my ribs. His hands are those of someone who works, but there's still softness to him.

With every sweeping movement down my body I felt closer to madness.

His body is pressed against mine. He is smooth against my back, yet hard like a wall made of stone. I don't know when his shirt came off and I don't care. I want more of him. He unfastens my jeans and they slide to the floor. The velvety softness of his underwear pressed against the thin strip of my panties. Even contained, he still feels so big.

I want to talk to tell the visions I'm having of him with his face between my legs or me in front of him, my hands resting on his muscular thighs as he slams into my throat, but the words are lost.

My pants are bunched around my ankles and my boots are still on. I still haven't touched him yet, not with my hands, but I know he's down to his skivvies as well. His hands are moving all over me now. One of them is flat against my wetness, while his other hand is moving up my body, over my small breasts, my sternum.

I lose my breath as his hand tightens around my throat.

"And you thought instead of waiting for me, you would play pretend?"

He squeezes against the moan trying to escape me. One of his fingers is pushing my thong between my lips. I feel myself dripping down my own thigh.

"I'm so disappointed in you, Sabby."

My body quakes beneath his weight. He releases some of the pressure and I take a greedy breath.

"I had something I wanted you to unwrap. Something special to stuff your stocking with."

His voice trails off. He's still touching me, driving me insane. I shift my weight, hoping to guide his hand. His grip tightens, pulling the back of my head against his chest as he applies pressure.

"You did good, telling me the truth. Good girls tell the truth. Don't they?"

I try to nod. He's still behind me. He has me held in place, and I love it. A smile warms his face, illuminating the deep tones of green in his eyes.

"I'm going to let you go," he says. My body relaxes as he does, but not even a breath has passed as I wish he was back on me, holding me, touching me, anything as long as it means I can feel him. "And you're going to sit on the floor and wait for me to tell you when you can unwrap your present."

I drop to the floor, using my jeans as a makeshift seat. Sexy Santa or not, I still have enough wherewithal to want to avoid sitting on the mall floor.

He steps around me. The first thing I see is the clear definition chiseled into his thigh; roughly the size of my head and if they're not made of stone, they have to be made of steel. Poking out several inches between his thighs as he walks is a deep red velvet thong trimmed with white fur. It matches the hat he's wearing. His chest is as smooth as the skin under his eyes and he is covered in tattoos.

I want to trace them all with my tongue, learn what each of them is and what they mean to him. Mostly I want to remove that piece of velvet and choke myself on his candy cane.

"Sit on your hands, Sabby."

My head tilts like our bulldog's noggin does when he's confused. He wanted me down here to unwrap a present and now he wants me to sit on my hands. I shift my weight to the front and raise my butt far enough off the ground to place my hands underneath.

He is glorious. I can't wait to run my fingers along his body. If he doesn't let me touch him soon I might go mad and lunge myself forward just to taste him. The saltiness of cured meats and the fiery pull of tequila permeate my mouth. This man's cock has me salivating.

"Your hands got you in trouble before, touching things that belong to me." He licks the inside of his hand, the one that was pressed against my center. "But your mouth told the truth, earning you a taste of what good girls get. Go ahead. Use your mouth to unwrap your present."

I lick my own lips and exhale sitting straighter. My tongue traces the edge along his thigh. Then I move to the next one. I stop for a minute with my mouth agape in front of the head of his cock. Following instructions, not wanting my present to be taken away before I even have a chance to play with it, I work my tongue under the edge and pull the fabric into my mouth. Once I have a grip on it I tug down like a lioness ripping off meat from a bone. It slides down but gets caught on his hardness.

Shifting I work the other side until finally he springs free, bouncing against my chin as he stands firm and erect. I sit up to admire his peppermint stick.

A small bead glistens on the tip. I look up past the ridges of muscle and into his eyes. I don't have to speak, my eyes are pleading enough for me. He smirks, and my body responds. My eyes wander down his body again stopping at the top of his pelvic bone where a roughly lined drawing of mistletoe is inked.

Even if he doesn't answer, I'm taking it as a sign to proceed. If I'm wrong he'll punish me, and bad girls can have just as much fun as good ones. If I'm right, I'll have the pleasure of tasting his precum.

My mouth lines up with his head and my tongue swirls against the small opening. He gasps and with no warning slams himself against my throat. I gag, tears fill my eyes and my throat constricts. He makes small, harsh thrusts, into the lining of my esophagus.

I want to grab his thighs, dig my nails into him to push him away and pull him in closer. I'm not even being touched and again I'm close to my own delight.

He grunts and moans as I move my tongue along his shaft. He can't fit all of himself in my mouth, but that's not stopping him from trying.

He pulls out slowly. Long strands of saliva hang between his shaft and my lips. I lick them up.

"That mouth of yours is a star," he says hungrily. "One I love having to top my wood."

It's a terrible pun, but if it means he's going to choke me with his cock again then it's my favorite pun in the whole world.

"Did you like that."

It wasn't a question. Before I can answer he's back inside my mouth. Something has slid between my legs. I can't see what it is, but it's thick.

"It feels like you did," he growls.

The thing moving between my thighs seems to be the lower part of his leg. I slide forward trying to line myself as flat against him as I can from this angle.

"Are you going to grind yourself against my leg?"

I stop moving my body, sure to keep the back and forth rhythm I had going with my head and neck. He is still pumping aggressively, each thrust trying to get further, deeper.

"Are you a bad little bitch or a good girl?"

Frankly, I am sure I can be both, but I don't know which is the right answer. I just know that I want to choke on him until we both cum and I'm so filled with his eggnog it leaks from my mouth.

His hands move to my neck. One is pressed against the front and the other is tangled in the base of my hair.

There is a swift pinch of pain. The air moves around me, something cold is against my ass and my back. In front of me is a wall of toned, tatted skin. A deep reservoir above a pronounced collar bone and a mountain of muscles above that. He's holding my neck, my toes grazing the floor. I'm too turned on to be scared. It hurts so good I'm sure I've come a little.

"Which are you, Sabby?"

"I'm a good girl," I say, forcing the words out. Blood is rushing through my body and I'm not sure how much of it is making it to my head. I'm no longer sure my toes are still able to reach the floor.

"Louder Sabby. I need to know that you understand."

"I'm your good girl, Santa."

His hands move and I can breathe. My body slides down until I'm straddling his knee. I look at his face, the room swirls behind him, his eyes are glued to mine, but I can feel his fingers gripping their way up my thighs. My boots and jeans are off. The only thing between us is a thin cotton thong that is beyond soaked.

"Oh yes, Sabby, you certainly are my good girl."

He lowers himself until he is eye level with my center. His hands pull me close to the edge of what seems to be a desk. I'm still not sure how I got from my knees to a seated position, but the only thing I'm upset about is that he's not the seat.

"Do you know what good girls taste like?"

I shake my head. My breath is shaky and I gasp as his finger runs up my slit. His touch is physically cold and yet I'm on fire.

He waves his other fingers under my nose, down onto my lips, parting them as he slides them into my mouth.

"Like egg yolks, sugar, and sweet wine," he chuckles softly.

I swallow. Before I can process what he's said, I feel myself stretching out over him. His two fingers practically filled my mouth, and I can only imagine what two of his fingers pressed inside of me will do. Already I'm rapidly falling to the edge and he's only using one.

His fingers work their way deeper into my throat, I gag and he takes his fingers from my mouth and begins working my clit like a mini joystick. My body is melting against his. With each wave of ecstasy, I can feel myself letting go.

"Come for me Sabby, cover me with your juices."

He puts a second finger inside me, still manipulating my clit with the hand from my mouth. My eyes roll as my head falls back. I do what he says. Somewhere far off I can hear the sound of rain hammering down onto the floor.

"Santa didn't know Sabby was a squirter."

His hat brushes against my legs as he laps at me. He sits up straighter, his fingers so deep inside me, his palm is flat against me. The tops of his knuckles pressing against my rim.

"What a good girl, letting Santa have a taste."

I lift my head and try to keep my eyes on his. Everything is swimming in and out of focus, I can feel and that's about it. I'm not sure what he's doing, but it has me moaning. My eyes close and my head lulls back again.

"Look at me," he commands. "Focus on me."

I try, but my eyes keep closing. I see his face, his chin is shiny as light reflects off the mess I've made, and then all I see are my eyelids.

"Sabby, look at me. Now," he warns. "Whose pussy is this?"

"Yours" I breathe. "Santa's"

"Such a good girl," he moans as he rips my panties off. The pinch of fabric pushes me closer even though his fingers are no longer inside me.

His hands are behind me, sprawled out across my back and my ass. Again I'm in the air but this time when I touch ground it's warm and fuzzy. I'm on my hands and knees. The floor is red with white trim. It feels amazing against my skin.

I lower myself so my forearms are flush with the floor. My knees are spread hip wide apart. His fingers gather in my hair guiding my head so it's facing forward.

"I'm going to fuck this perfect pussy until you scream my name."

Tension is building inside me. I'm going to come too quickly, I want to say something but before I can, I feel the head of his cock pressed against my walls. The only sounds I'm able to make are feral.

I feel myself being split down the middle as he enters me. He keeps my head pulled back with his grip on my hair.

"Keep squeezing me tighter, pull me into you."

I'm panting, breathlessly crying out. When he's fully seated inside me I've already come at least once. I don't know how much more I can take. He leans forward. His breath wet against my ear.

"You like having me inside you, Sabby?"

"Yes, Santa," I moan.

The slightest movement of his throbbing cock inside me sends tremors through my body.

"I think you've earned being on the Nice List this year. So now I'm going to fuck you like the dirty little slut you are, Sabby."

I shudder, already I feel myself adjusting to his size as I slowly shift back and forth.

"Whose dirty little slut are you?"

He pulls out a little, there's still so much of him inside me. I can't speak. He slides a little further out.

"I won't ask again. Whose. Dirty. Little. Slut. Are. You."

Is it really a question if we both know the answer?

"Santa's," I cry out as he slams the full length of himself inside me.

He rides me like this, with one hand alternating between being wrapped around my throat or tangled in my hair while the other grips my hip bone using it for leverage. Occasionally he spanks my ass sending sparks across my body. I buck like a wild horse. I scream and cry out, moaning unintelligibly until he flips me over.

He stuffs something underneath me and pulls me closer. My hips are in the air, my pussy wide open and dripping wet for him. He leans forward and runs his tongue from my taint to the tip of my slit.

"If we had more time, I would devastate you. Leave you utterly broken for any man but me. Such a beautiful and stunning creature you are, Sabby."

My jaw is quivering and I still can't see straight as he pushes inside of me. Through my fluttering eyelashes I can see his body working as he drives into me. The looks of pleasure and hunger dance across his face.

"I'm going to fill you with my come until it drips out," he growls.

"Yes please," I moan.

His tongue runs itself along the inside of my ankle as his hands pinch my nipples. There's a pull low and heavy building inside of me.

"Choke me, Santa. Choke me until you come," I gasp.

He's driving into me, his tattooed body stimulating my clit as he thrusts full inside me. Both his hands are wrapped around my neck. The pressure is surreal. His beautiful devilish eyes lock on mine. The world around him is graying and suddenly I feel him shoot against me, my own body pulsating in response.

He releases his grip on my throat and I scream out "Santa, Daddy!"

Everything is vibrating. It feels like a million Christmas mornings at once. Complete and utter joy have taken over. We lay there for a minute next to each other. His fingers lightly tickling the side of my thigh.

"Holy shit," I finally whisper.

"I believe you're looking for Holy Night."

I turn my head to the side. He's just as handsome when he's not rearranging my internal organs. He's also funny.

"Did you say something about time?"

I start to panic when he hands me my phone.

"Thank you" I mutter.

Three texts, all within the last five minutes. I breathe out a sigh of relief.

"Everything's okay."

He says it like he already knows the answer.

"Yeah. My parents need some more time so they're letting my brother see a movie with his friends. Operation Secret Santa is still a go."

I blush and look at him closely. It's hard to place his age, probably in his 40s, but he could be younger or older. I really don't care, so I don't ask.

"Can I be your secret Santa?"

"I believe you already are."

He winks. I wink back before rolling my eyes.

"One question before I head back. There's no unions for Santas, they keep us on a tight schedule."

I sit up waiting to hear what he's going to ask. My feet are crossed underneath me and I'm definitely slouching, but I'm comfortable emotionally and physically. I decide to embrace it instead of worrying.

"If you could have any*thing* for Christmas, what would it be?"

My eyebrow shoots up. This is his question. Not can I have your number, do you want me to rail you again, not even are you on birth control since I just shot my load — my mind goes still, but before I get lost in my thoughts, I feel his warmth around my knee. His hand is there, his thumb already making small circles.

"Any present in the world. Think rules of the Genie," he continues.

"Okay," I offer a soft laugh.

My heart swims for a moment in the memories I have of my mother before she died. Not that I would wish for her back, I miss her, but if she was back I wouldn't have Bastion in my life. It's just not possible to choose between your mother and your brother, at least not for me, so I don't.

"Don't I have to sit on your lap for this? Or since there are rules, do you have a lamp I should rub?"

"If you sit on me, I'd prefer it to be my face, and we definitely don't have time for that or for you to rub my lamp, which coincidentally—" His voice trails off. Again I feel a smile spread across my face. If we did have more time he would already be ready.

"An English Christmas," I hear myself say. "Somewhere where they'll get snow, preferably the countryside. Just me and a bunch of books and a ton of hot chocolate. Maybe not on actual Christmas, but yeah. That."

"No boyfriend — or err — girlfriend? No family? No friends?"

"I'm not opposed to sharing that with someone, but as of right now, I don't have anyone special enough to share that with."

"No one?"

"No one I'm aware of."

I laugh, mostly in surprise that I would say something so clingy and corny and hopeful, maybe?

"I'll see what I can do, I am Santa after all and we've already established that you are definitely on the nice list."

# Three

A week has passed since Sebastian and I went and got our picture taken with Santa. Fucker has officially ruined the holiday for me.

In addition to having bought a new half glass, half silicone s-shaped vibrator appropriately named Kris Kringle, I also have replayed our tryst countless times. Every day I thank God Kris is rechargeable because I'm sure I would have run through all the batteries Susan and my dad keep in the emergency kit.

I also haven't heard from him, something I usually wouldn't mind. A one time thing is a one time thing, but everywhere I look there's another red suited, white bearded Santa jingling his bells and spreading his jolly. Before I know it I'm wet and gooey even when it's *not* him, and it never is. Not that I'm obsessing or anything.

Emma shot me questioning looks throughout our entire breakfast and both Susan and my dad have asked in private if there's anyone new in my life.

Most people assume Sabby is my given name, and when they realize it's actually, Zabaglione, they can't fathom how to pronounce it. Yet somehow he knew it was my name and what it tasted like. Just like he seemed to know exactly what to do to me.

Oh god, the noises I made. Heat flushes my face and I feel the heaviness start. I look at the alarm clock on the table. There's not enough time to replay the whole scene in my head before I have to be downstairs for Christmas breakfast and presents.

Not even *I'm* that selfish to make my family delay the festivities for me to have my hundredth orgasm this week. Though I was late for dinner two nights ago.

I sigh and force myself up and out of bed, throwing on the Christmas pajama set that Susan left in my room last night. Thankfully she did it when Bastian and I were cleaning up dinner and not after. She would have been in for a shocking surprise had she snuck in last night; since while the rest of my family was having homemade whipped cream topped hot chocolate and freshly baked cookies for dessert, I was thinking about Santa whipping me as his cream glazed my cookie.

Before leaving my room I plug Kris Kringle for later. Better to be satisfied to the Nth degree than have to wait for the power to be recharged.

Everyone is already sitting in the living room by the time I walk in. We're each allowed to open one gift from Santa before breakfast. Bastian's younger so I let him go first.

Our parents got him a spot at some winter sports camp. You have to be a talented kid to get in, and Bastian definitely is, but the committee is super selective. When letters came around Bastian got a fake one, written by yours truly, rejecting him. The kid was heartbroken, but handled it like a champ, which made the sacrifice of offering my Christmas budget to go to his haul even more worth it. It was one thing to get to go to the camp, but it was a Christmas spectacular for him to get all new equipment too.

This also meant that whatever is under this tree from Santa (ie: my parents) will be heartfelt but small potatoes. Not that I mind, I have enough crap as it is. I look at the pile figuring it's best to start with the small of the small, I don't want Bastian to get even a whiff of the tom foolery our parents had set up. They spent all of yesterday setting up this epic Christmas scavenger hunt for him, all while he was at his friends for a Christmas party and I was getting off in my car thinking about the Big Guy in red himself, or at least one of the approximately 2 million mall Santas in this country.

Bastian's still whooping it up over the new console he unwrapped. My father and Susan look at me as my brother is showing it off to our 100 year old bulldog, Maverick. I smile and shrug.

There's a card with my name on it. I figure that's small enough. I ignore the looks my dad and Susan seem to be exchanging. They probably can't believe I managed to score the console for him, or at least are trying to figure out what I did to pay for it. In this case, the less they know the better.

The card is simple: an idyllic country scene dusted with snow and a tiny cottage with a chimney with large billows of smoke coming off the top. Inside was the same handwriting, not as large, but just as pretty.

*An English Christmas filled with books, hot cocoa, & surprises*
*Spring Break, next year*
*Merry Christmas, Sabby*
*- Santa*

"What did you get Sabby? Just a card?!" Bastian says running over to me.

"I told Santa that you didn't really get arrested and that you weren't bad at all. Does it say why you only got a card?"

I look up to him, the sincerity in his face is almost enough to distract me. My eyes shift over to our parents, who are just as curious as and confused as Bastian.

"Apparently Santa got me an English Christmas in March..." I wait for a spark of anything in either of their faces. "Literally what I've always wanted," I continue.

Finally my dad walks over, "let me see that." He and Susan look at it closely. Tucked in the envelope is a plane ticket—for first freaking business class—and the name of the limo company that will be taking me to my cottage. I'm in actual shock. My body is cold, my brain is on fire.

It's a full minute before I realize I haven't said anything. Bastian is already back to examining his gaming thing and Maverick is already asleep, again. Susan is smiling to herself, but she's always doing that. She's already halfway to the kitchen with my dad in tow before I stand up.

"Wait," I say. I run up to both of them, I lower my voice even though I don't think my brother will hear. "Thank you guys! Really, it's too much. Thank you."

Before they can respond, I pull both of them into a hug. Dad's eyes are already welling up as I break off and head back upstairs to find my phone.

There's one new text from SANTA 🎅:

> It's the busiest time of year for my family, my brothers and I are learning the tricks of the trade as they say. Haven't had a moment to reach out. I'll be free in March. See you then, Sabby.

> In the meantime, give that toy a break, and don't forget whose good girl you really are. . .

There's no contact information. Before I think to grab a screenshot, it's gone. I steal a glance at Kris Kringle, charged and ready for action. Maybe I've been having too much of a good time this past week. Can too many orgasms deprive the brain of vital oxygen?

Susan calls upstairs. Breakfast will be ready in a few. I open my laptop and check the flight details and the limo company. It's all real. *His brothers*—could he be real?

My whole body tingles at the thought of who might be joining me. I roll my eyes and look at my computer screen. Merry Christmas to me!

# Want More?

# About the Author

**Libby Scores** is a lot of things, including a writer of smut.

To learn more about her and the rest of the holiday series of
naughty novellas:
https://www.easeverything.com/

*Thank you for reading!!!*

www.ingramcontent.com/pod-product-compliance
Lightning Source LLC
Chambersburg PA
CBHW070753180626
46818CB00007B/3095